PLANTATION TALES COLLECTION

BWWM EROTICA COLLECTION

PLANTATION SEX TALES BOOKS 1-3

SAGE DEARLY

TWINFUL PLEASURES

BWWM HISTORICAL SHORT

FOREWORD

Thanks for picking up this quick read collection. The Plantation Sex Tales collection is historical, sexy, and, explicit, featuring an unspoiled black woman and white men.

I assume you are at least 18 years old if you're reading this.

If you enjoy it, make sure to sign up for my mailing list.

Thanks again,
Sage.

CHAPTER 1

*S*omething significant began in Vaneeta's young life in the Savannah plantation during the year 1857, marking a pivotal moment.

The sun bore down relentlessly on the sprawling plantation.

The heat that was cast mercilessly over the cotton fields was so intense that it made it difficult for the slaves to toil, while the overseers kept a watchful eye on them.

Among the slaves, the young woman stood out in the sea of black, sweat-filled faces.

Her captivating beauty was not the only thing that made her admirable, but also her spirit that seemed to resist the surrounding oppression.

Vaneeta, who had just turned eighteen, was her given name. Her round face was framed by a crown of thick, curly, kinky, afro, and which highlighted her unique charm that was a rarity in those parts.

She managed to maintain a well-rested appearance

despite putting in the same amount of effort as her fellow slaves.

Most of the negroes on the plantation were utterly defeated, resulting in their faces bearing the marks of their sadness and causing them to appear hopeless, which was unappealing.

Her striking features, however, were a double-edged sword, because they attracted both the admiration of fellow slaves and the unwanted attention of the white men who owned them.

In spite of the fact that she had provoked none of them, some women accused her of being too uppity and thinking she was better than them.

The cotton fields stretched out before her, and she appeared as a figure of grace and elegance as she moved through them in her simple, worn-out and faded white dress.

The cotton was plucked from its boll with great precision and care by her nimble fingers, which moved deftly and with skill.

She had been doing this for the entirety of her life, and it had become almost mechanical to her.

The dress, being one of only three that she owned, was something she treasured and treated with care.

Knowing that her destiny, just like all other slaves, was restricted by the chains of servitude, she felt a sense of hopelessness. There was no escaping her life on the plantation.

The place of her pappy's birth was also the place where he drew his last breath, right there on the plantation.

After the death of her father by hanging, she watched as her mother aged rapidly before her very eyes.

Despite his repeated denials, they refused to believe him when he was accused of stealing.

Someone finally came forward and confessed to the theft, but it was too late because it happened seven months to the day after his death. Because of a debt that needed to be settled, one of the young sons of the plantation owner stole the small statue.

That they had hanged an innocent man didn't seem to matter to them. Ma wasn't even offered an apology by anyone. The memory of that moment never left her, even though she was just a young girl.

It was a couple of years later when the plantation was sold and they were left with a new master.

The new owner, Master James, was considerably younger than his predecessor and, besides that, he had a kind face.

Most of the slaves under his ownership were treated kindly by him, and sometimes he could be found in the fields alongside them, picking cotton.

Vaneeta was attracted to him because of his good looks and found him to be quite handsome despite the age difference.

Lately, her thoughts about him had become unpure. Even after spending time in prayer regarding them, the thoughts remained and didn't seem to go away.

She was cautious not to spend too much time with him, as she didn't want to disclose her emotions and feelings. Surely, he would notice.

Vaneeta persisted with her work, even though her

body ached, and her soul longed for freedom. She knew that the overseer, a cruel and watchful man, kept a close eye on her.

Whenever he looked at her with his leering gaze, her skin would crawl with disgust, and she had become accustomed to tolerating his disturbing presence solely to escape the cruel lash of the whip.

Vaneeta's mind often wandered to dreams of a life beyond the plantation. She dared to imagine a world where she could live freely, where her fate was her own to decide.

She couldn't help but wonder if there was a parallel world where the life she yearned for was a reality, or was she fated to live out her days in her current world?

She was always cautious about dreaming, knowing full well that such dreams were dangerous and could be shattered by the harsh realities of her enslaved existence. Even dreaming about freedom was dangerous in her world.

She had seen the fate of those who dared to challenge their lot. Some were sold off to faraway plantations, torn from their families and everything they knew.

Others faced a different but equally daunting future; becoming the property of some white man who desired a slave for more than just labor. The stories were plenty.

The thought made her shudder with fear and disgust. She had caught glimpses of how men, both black and white, eyed her with desire. Their lustful stares made her feel vulnerable and objectified.

Vaneeta was determined to remain inconspicuous, to wear her simple dresses and avoid attracting attention.

Yet, she knew that no matter how modestly she dressed, the men's eyes would always follow her.

Little did she know that fate had its own plans for her, plans that would set her on a path she could never have imagined.

As she worked, she noticed the handsome plantation owner, Mr. James, approaching the field.

Her heart raced because of her secret crush, and she knew such feelings were forbidden and dangerous.

Trying to distract her mind, she raised her hand and appealed for consent to take a small restroom break.

The overseer grunted his approval, telling her to be quick about it.

"You want some company?" he leered as he grabbed his crotch and licked his lips, leaving no doubt his intentions.

With his ugly, cackling laughter ringing in her ears, Vaneeta ran towards the latrine as fast as she could.

Her emotional state was in disarray, with conflicting feelings all jumbled together.

After making sure that no one was watching, she tiptoed towards the latrine and then looked through the open window.

There, inside, was Master James, dressed in a dapper shirt and vest, with brown trousers. His fly was down and his cock peeked out as it let out a powerful stream of pee.

She caught a full view of it from her vantage point, and she felt herself get wet as her knees buckled. It looked thick and strong, nothing like she'd ever seen before, and her eyes grew wide.

She wished she could pleasure herself like she sometimes did when she had one of the rare moments of solitude.

No man had ever possessed her, but she knew she wanted Master James badly.

Her quick reflexes saved her and she ducked just in time because he suddenly glanced her way.

CHAPTER 2

$\mathscr{E}$xcitement buzzed around the plantation like a swarm of bees. Vaneeta had never witnessed a day like this before, as it was the grand celebration of Master James's birthday.

The word of the approaching celebration had circulated rapidly, creating a buzz among the slaves, who were both excited and apprehensive about what the event might entail.

The day promised to be an exciting one, and as the sun rose, the main mansion was already bustling with activity and preparations.

Under the direction of Miss Berna, the head maid, the enslaved workers worked tirelessly to decorate the house in the finest fashion possible, ensuring every detail was perfect.

The decoration team went all out, covering the walls with colorful balloons, hanging elegant drapes, and placing fragrant flowers in every corner to create a beautiful setting.

The mansion was transformed into an opulent spectacle that was reserved only for special occasions, and it completely changed the atmosphere inside.

Vaneeta was unaware at the time, but later found out that the master was turning 35, marking a significant milestone.

Among the various preparations, the slaves joined forces to bake a massive cake.

Flour, sugar, and eggs combined with team effort, and they created a delightful confection that seemed to tower over everything else in the room.

It was the biggest, grandest cake Vaneeta had ever seen. The tantalizing aroma of the freshly baked cake wafted through the air, making her mouth water.

In honor of the master's birthday, barrels of alcohol were brought to the mansion, ready to be consumed throughout the day's revelry. It was an indulgence rarely seen on the plantation.

The men folk in the slaves' quarters quickly claimed several bottles that were even delivered to them. Drinking something different from their usual homemade moonshine was a pleasant change for them.

Much to their surprise, the slaves were granted a rare day off from their grueling labor.

It was a gesture unheard of under the previous master's rule. The old master was harsh and merciless, showing no compassion for his slaves, but it seemed Master James held a different perspective.

Many of them had known nothing but cruelty and oppression, so this change in the atmosphere was both refreshing and unsettling.

Just before the party began, unexpected visitors arrived at the plantation. It was a Master William, another plantation owner, and the twin brother of Mr. James. They were nearly identical, with the same striking features, except for one distinction.

The two gentlemen, Master William and Master James, had contrasting facial hair styles with Mr. William being clean-shaven and Mr. James sporting a closely cropped beard.

Due to the fact that he lived far away from Savannah, the two brothers seldom had the opportunity to see each other.

Vaneeta was taken aback and couldn't believe what she was seeing before her very eyes. The sight of Mr. William, so eerily similar to the master of the plantation, left her momentarily shocked.

The question that lingered in her thoughts was whether the two brothers' treatment and values towards their slaves were similar or not.

She also couldn't help but wonder if they shared everything else as her mind flashed back to seeing Master James in the latrine.

As the evening drew near, the festivities unfolded. Men and women who were impeccably dressed made their way to the plantation, arriving in a magnificent assortment of horses, buggies, and coaches.

All the slaves wore their Sunday Church outfits as they had been instructed to, even though their celebration was confined to their quarters.

The laughter and music filled the air, momentarily lifting the weight of servitude from the slaves' shoulders.

While everyone was enjoying the merriment, Vaneeta quietly left and made her way to the main house.

She peered through the crowd inside until her eyes found the two masters.

Observing the twin brothers, she tried to discern differences in their demeanor.

While Master James seemed to enjoy the attention and admiration of the crowd, Master William appeared more reserved and contemplative.

She reckoned it was because of his distance from home and being among strangers.

Amidst the grand celebration, the time had come for Mr. James and Mr. William to cut their magnificent birthday cake. With its intricate icing and towering height that seemed to reach the ceiling, the cake stood as the main centerpiece in the opulent hall of the main mansion.

The brothers' resemblance was so striking that it was clear they were twins as they stood shoulder to shoulder.

Guests gathered around the table, their eyes gleaming with excitement, as the brothers prepared to cut the cake. Master James, with a broad smile, gripped the knife in his hand.

"To another year of prosperity and happiness," he proclaimed, raising his glass of wine high.

The sentiment was echoed by all the guests, who raised their glasses in unison. The room was filled with a chorus of cheers as the two brothers cut into the cake, celebrating the occasion.

Amid the revelry, Vaneeta couldn't resist the temptation to sneak a glimpse from the outside.

The sight of the jubilant crowd and the happiness

within the mansion captivated her young mind. It was a different world.

Her heart pounded in her chest as she glanced through the window, trying to remain hidden from view.

In a stroke of ill fate, her eyes met those of Master William, who had caught her spying. A sly smile crept across his face, a glint of intrigue in his eyes.

Fear and curiosity collided within Vaneeta. Instinct told her to run away and seek safety, yet an inexplicable magnetism held her in place.

She couldn't comprehend Master William's intentions, and that uncertainty unsettled her.

As the cake-cutting ceremony continued inside, Vaneeta hesitated, unsure of what to do. But to her surprise, Mr. William slipped away from the gathering and approached her cautiously.

"You seem curious, my dear," he mumbled, the smile still playing at the corner of his lips.

Vaneeta's heart raced, but she found the courage to respond. "I didn't mean to intrude, sir. I was just watching. Please don't punish me, Sir," her voice pleading.

With a slight chuckle; "No need to apologize. Besides, I find your boldness quite charming."

Not wanting to seem intrusive, he kept to himself the fact that he had noticed her when his carriage had drawn up earlier in the day.

Vaneeta's cheeks heated with a mix of embarrassment and uncertainty. She had never been addressed in such a manner by a white man before, and it both intrigued and alarmed her.

"I should get back to my room, Master William Sir,"

she mumbled as she attempted to distance herself from the enigmatic plantation owner.

The master's eyes softened as he spoke. "There's no hurry, because tonight is a night of celebration for everyone."

The warmth in his voice puzzled Vaneeta, who expected hostility and indifference from a man in his position.

Yet, here he was, standing before her with an air of familiarity that defied the norms of their society.

As the night breeze gently rustled the leaves of the nearby trees, Master William leaned against a wooden post, his eyes never leaving Vaneeta's face. "Tell me," he asked, "do you dream of more?"

"I can't afford to dream, Master Sir." She said it in a plain voice after a long pause, a trace of sadness in her voice.

Vaneeta's heart skipped a beat. She hadn't expected such a question, nor had she expected opening up to a man who, despite his charm, was still a part of the oppressive system that kept her enslaved.

"I... I do dream of freedom," she stuttered as she uttered the words, her voice soft and uncertain.

Master William's smile remained, but there was a touch of empathy in his gaze. "Sometimes, there are things you can do to make life easier. You are an exquisite creature" His gaze fell to her breasts as he spoke and the desire was unmistakable.

Vaneeta felt the heat rise within her as her nipples hardened.

He continued: "Would you like to give me and my brother a special birthday gift?"

Vaneeta's eyes widened, her mind struggling to comprehend his words. Before she could respond, Master William held up a finger, signaling for her to wait.

"Meet me at the front door, after the festivities have ended. It's your choice," he said before he strode back into the house, his coattails flapping in the wind, which allowed her to see the well-defined outline of his buttocks.

Vaneeta's heart raced as she nodded to herself, her decision already made and, her mind swirling with anticipation and trepidation.

Master William turned around once more and smiled before stepping inside the door. "There is much more to celebrate," he mouthed to himself.

Vaneeta watched him disappear into the revelry, her heart in tumult.

She straightened up and ran her hand over her skirt, her mind made up. She wanted to give them the special gift.

CHAPTER 3

*A*fter the jubilant celebration had ended and the guests departed, the plantation mansion fell into a hushed stillness.

Vaneeta, her heart pounding, returned as requested to meet with Master William, the enigmatic brother of Master James.

Vaneeta took a moment to gather herself, inhaling deeply, before she summoned the courage to knock on the grand oak door of the mansion.

Standing outside, she could feel the coolness of the night air against her skin, and the stars that shimmered above her looked like distant diamonds.

She was still dressed in her Sunday finest because she wanted to look her best. Except for her hat, everything else seemed in place, and her large afro swayed slightly in the wind.

With a creaking sound, the door slowly opened and revealed Master James standing there with a warm smile on his face, ready to greet her.

"Thank you for coming, Vaneeta," he said graciously, inviting her inside.

As soon as Vaneeta stepped inside the main house, she was momentarily awestruck by what she saw, as this was the first time she had ever set foot in such a luxurious place.

The opulence and grandeur of the place were unlike anything she had ever seen. Rich tapestries adorned the walls, elegant chandeliers hung from the ceilings, and ornate furniture filled the rooms.

The main room, which was decorated with various items, had a focal point that was designed to catch everyone's attention, namely the head of a buck with antlers that was displayed in the center of the room.

Vaneeta tried to hide her amazement as she followed Master James through the spacious hallway.

Her apprehension was clear as she balled her hands into tight fists to find some relief.

Master James led her to one of the guest bedrooms at the rear of the house. His brother trailed behind, having joined them.

As they walked on the soft, plush carpet, their footsteps were completely silent, allowing them to make their way without making any noise.

The room had a tasteful decoration, with various shades of red.

"Please, have a seat," he offered, gesturing towards a plush chair near the window. "My brother and I are thrilled you took us up on the offer."

Vaneeta settled herself down in the chair, sitting in a prim and proper manner, while her heart continued to race in her chest.

Her eyes wandered around the room, taking in the details. The bed had fine linens and plush pillows, a stark contrast to the hard straw mattress she was accustomed to.

Although the room was beautiful, her sudden doubts lingered and provided no ease.

Masters James and William moved closer to her, their eyes traveling up and down her body, lingering on her curves and soft contours.

She felt heat darken her cheeks as she met their gaze, embarrassed but also strangely drawn to them. It was almost as if her body was under their spell, and she couldn't look away even if she wanted to.

As they stood before her, the bulge in their trousers was more prominent, and she found her eyes drawn to them almost involuntarily.

The sight was captivating and oppressive in its intensity. She felt her breath quicken and her plain underwear became damp as she struggled to find the right words to say.

The Masters exchanged a knowing look of appreciation, and she felt her heart beat faster in anticipation of what was to come.

She was both excited and scared at the thought of being taken in by them both together.

"Do you like what you see?" It was Master James, and he was delighted by the look on her face. Vaneeta could only bob her head up and down because her mouth had gone dry.

"We're going to make sure that you enjoy our birthday

gift, too." He traced his fingers lightly over her lips as her mouth cracked open.

He looked into her eyes and leaned in closer till his face was just inches from her and she could feel the warm breath on her skin. Then he kissed her softly, causing a wave of pleasure to ripple through her body.

"I love her thick cocoa lips, don't you, William?" He spoke between kisses as he tasted her saliva, his tongue darting into her willing orifice.

His brother nodded. He couldn't wait to taste them.

He tasted like honey and she didn't know how to respond at first, but reciprocated by instinct.

The musky cologne he was wearing filled her senses, and she couldn't help but find it incredibly sexy and enticing.

Master William asked in a soft voice, "Can we help you undress?" even though his hand had already removed one of her shoes.

She nodded once more since her mouth was occupied by Master James, who expertly relieved her of her blouse and corset till her breasts were exposed to their lust-filled eyes.

Master James then held the big, firm breasts in his hands, molding and pinching her nipples before popping one stiff one in his mouth while she moaned as she felt herself getting wetter.

"Does that feel good? Do your tits feel good stuffed in my mouth? Do you want more than my mouth?" he inquired as he licked away.

Vaneeta's heart skipped a beat, surprised by Master James's acknowledgment of her deepest yearning. "How did you know?" she stammered, her eyes searching his face for answers.

His voice was thick; "I've observed you for so long, my beautiful Vaneeta. All the negroes and everyone else on the plantation were warned to keep their paws offa you."

She felt a rush of raw emotion at knowing that he had noticed her all along. It all made sense to her now.

Most of the other slaves were deflowered by the time they were her age. She had been saved for the master, and it made her feel powerful , wanted, and relieved much of her worry.

She ventured timidly with a question that had been on her mind for a long time; "Was that why that nasty old man was beaten?" She had tried to find out what had happened, but no one knew.

It had happened one day as she was getting ready to leave the cotton field. She was sent to bring a jug of water to one overseer and was told to hurry.

With the filled jug in hand, she approached the modest shack that wasn't too far from the slaves' quarters.

She assumed she was bringing the water to one woman of the house, and was surprised when a gruff voice told her to come in. She stepped in with trepidation.

The silence was a clear sign that something was not right.

Her fear was confirmed upon entry. There, standing, was the man she and the rest of the negroes referred to as "Old meanie."

He was the wickedest of them and was quick with the whip, often whipping hard enough to tear open the skin and draw blood.

She had escaped his punishment. Until now.

He had arrived at the plantation about three months back and his reputation preceded him. Everyone feared him, and here she was, in his clutches.

"Git in here," he growled at her, jolting her out of her thoughts.

She stood frozen. The look in his eyes made her skin crawl. He was a short, stumpy man with rotten teeth that were stained yellow from tobacco. He was heavyset and had a long grey beard, and he smelled badly, a mixture of alcohol, tobacco, and dirty hygiene.

"I said git, before you get a taste of my whip." For good measure, he reached for it from the shelf and cracked it against the floor.

Crawling towards him with fear in her heart, her eyes filled with dread at the thought of what might happen.

"Take off your blouse and let me see those teats" His voice brooked no argument. She was powerless, such was the fate of a slave.

Just as her blouse was over her head, she heard some commotion in the room, and then silence.

She opened her eyes which she'd tightly shut, and he was gone. It was almost as if it had all been a dream.

Not bothering to find out happened, she ran as fast as her legs could carry her back to the safety of the slave's quarters.

Her whole body shook, and she had nightmares for weeks after, but she never spoke of it to anyone, until now.

"Yes, I had him beaten within an inch of his life because he dared to even look at you. One of the domestic slaves had seen and came to tell me. My blood boiled, and I wanted to kill him." His face grew red at the recollection.

"I'm glad you saved me, Master James." Her voice was full of gratitude. She was now even more willing to do anything he wanted. "I'm all yours." Her voice was husky and she meant it.

She never laid eyes on the Old meanie again, and nobody ever asked what happened to him. They were just glad he disappeared.

There were rampant rumors; He'd stolen something, he'd killed another white man and more, but she always suspected it had to do with that afternoon. Now she was sure.

The raw need was coursing through her veins like wildfire. "Take me as your own, Master James. I'm here for your pleasure."

Master William got on his knees then, and, with both hands, pushed her skirt all the way up around her thighs, kissing his way up her body, giving her goosebumps while she writhed.

He spread her legs apart and motioned to his brother.

"Look how perfect she is, our back beauty" he exclaimed, drawing back so his brother could see.

Both of them helped undress her then, each grabbing one side of her underwear, which was already wet, and slid them down her legs until she was fully exposed to their dancing eyes.

"She's got the most beautiful pussy I've ever seen. Don't you agree, James?" He held up the discarded underwear to his nostrils and inhaled deeply before slipping it into his pocket.

"I bet it's juicy too, judging by her wetness, and we ain't even done nothing," agreed Master James as he stared, pulling his trousers off at the same time.

Vaneeta had lost all modesty within seconds of being

naked. She was now feeling wanted and desired. There was power in her pussy and she opened wider so they could see all of her.

"What do you want, Vaneeta?" growled Mr. James as he stroked his dick, which seemed to have swollen to twice the size she had seen in the latrine. It looked angry, fleshy, and ready for action.

"I want you Master James. I want you." She breathed.

"Then tell me, tell me in the coarsest way possible, nothing dainty. Tell me exactly what you want," he commanded through gritted teeth.

"I want you to fuck me, Master. I want your big white cock buried in my black pussy." The words rushed out of her mouth unchecked.

She would have loved to touch herself, but both brothers were holding on to her hands as if they knew. Her body arched up as she pleaded.

"So, you're saying that my lobcock needs to be burrowed deep within your sweet untouched cunny?" His voice was rough and held promises soon to be delivered.

"Master James, Master Williams, I want you both to fuck my pussy till it's raw and flood me with your milky juice." Her breath was rapid, and every cell in her body tingled as she twisted.

"We can do anything we want with your body? Is that my understanding?" He was teasing her now, and she knew it.

"Anything you want. Anything. Just don't leave me hanging. I need you, masters. I need those juicy looking cocks" She knew she was beyond holding on to any shred of decorum, and she didn't care.

Master James and his brother then lifted her and settled her on the soft, plush carpet. One of them slid a cushion under her.

Once splayed like an eagle, Master William undressed with haste, moving towards Vaneeta's face, while Master James stared at her warm pussy before descending on it.

It was his house, and it was only proper that he went first.

The feel of his rough beard against her skin made her tingly, and she bucked from the excitement.

He held her legs wide apart and, with one hand, parted her slick wet folds dotted with baby hair.

His tongue darted into her pussy with gusto, slurping and licking at her entrails while she screamed.

"Go ahead, scream with pleasure all you want. No one's going to disturb the party," promised Master Williams as he swung his erect penis across her mouth before plunging it in to get it wet.

His manhood looked just as big as his brother's and she almost choked as it glided into her mouth.

Master James was still feasting on her pussy and she thought she would explode. She had never imagined such pleasure as she ground her hips to his mouth.

"No one's ever eaten your cunt, have they?" he questioned when he came up for air.

"No sir, Master James. Ain't no one has ever eaten this kitty, I promise." Her voice was squeaky as she grabbed his head, forcing it back to her wicked muff.

She enjoyed hearing the moans coming from both men because she was giving them equal pleasure. Her hands reached for her nipples.

She pinched and pulled at the stiff nobs to heighten her pleasure, and Master William quickly took over as his heavy balls dangled. She scratched at them playfully while he groaned.

At some point, Master James stopped eating her pussy, much to her disappointment, and she let him know as much; "Noooo, don't stop eating ma pussy, Master."

He taunted her; "Don't you fret, my black angel. Now comes the best part. Are you ready for the best darn banging of your life?"

"Yessir, master, I'm ready," she hissed as she thrust her hips up to him.

He grabbed her ankles and pushed them until they almost reached her chest.

His cock seemed even bigger, and she spied a little cum on the bulbous head.

He brought it to her entrance, rubbed the tip along her lips, wetting it even more, before he slipped the head inside the tight hole.

Her breath caught sharply at the slight pain it caused, and she reared up. She had some doubt about being able to take in his immense cock, and she let out a pitiful whimper. He would split her wide apart, she thought.

Sensing her discomfort, Master James paused for a minute till she got used to the blunt invader.

Master Williams offered words of encouragement; "You're doing just fine. It's going to feel real good in a minute. I'm gonna fuck those big jugs of yours in the meantime while my brother breaches your entrails," he said as he pulled his cock out of her mouth and slid it between her breasts, which he squished together.

Vaneeta watched in a trancelike state as he slid in and out between her breasts. Sometimes, he came up far enough that she could lick at it, and it became a mission to taste it before it disappeared again.

It took her mind off her pussy and Master James drilled a little deeper, taking delight in feeling the tight pussy that was being stretched by his powerful weapon, and ground into her in a circular motion.

He began spearing into her as she relaxed. Every inch gained felt like he was conquering a new territory.

For Vaneeta, the pain gave way to intense pleasure, and she soon responded to the masterful strokes as her pussy widened to receive him.

He had grabbed on to her ass and was drilling with all his might while his brother fucked her teats.

All the wonderful sensations welled up within her ad the blood rushed to her head and she howled like a banshee. Something was happening. Was she about to die?

"I'm gonna explode." She yelled at the top of her lungs to no-one in particular. The next second, a wave washed over her and she experienced the first orgasm of her life.

Her juices mixed with those of Master James, who, after more unrelenting pounding, was all the way deep in her womb. His cock fitted like a glove within her folds. He saw Vaneeta's face and knew she was about to drench his cock with her climax.

He held her in a vice like grip to keep from being ejected from her well, and when his eruption came just seconds later, his cum gushed out like a geyser as he flooded her cunt with his load. A primal scream erupted from deep in his belly.

Master Williams, who had held on for as long as he could, drenched her breasts and face with his essence. All three fell to the floor panting.

Master James left, then returned shortly afterwards with some cool water to refresh them.

They rested very little before they changed places and she got serviced by Master William, who had her kneeling on the floor while he ravaged her from behind.

He was just as skillful as his brother. She almost preferred that position because the slap of his balls in her nether region felt great and heightened her sensation.

Master James was fondling her breasts, which dangled in front of him like two big, beautiful watermelons, he said.

She desperately wished she could suck his cock, but had to settle for gripping it as she fisted the stone-like appendage up and down till he finally relented and drove it deep in her mouth, his hands entangled in her afro as he thrust his hips fast and furious.

"Swallow it whole. Swallow my entire cock deep in that sweet mouth. You feel so good. Does it feel good to you, too?"

"Yes, master, it does. I feel you deep in my throat."

"But you loved everything we've done to you so far?"

"Yes, yes, I do."

"And you want me to come in that tight cherry mouth of yours, don't you?"

She was delirious; "Come on me, anywhere you like. My mouth, my tight black pussy, my tits, it's all yours for the taking, Master James."

"How does my white cock taste?" He had a deep desire to know.

"The taste is tangy, like fresh honey mixed with salt. My throat is raw, but I love your big white cock in it." Her body was wracked with sobs as she took the fierce pounding, both in her mouth and pussy.

The whole of her being was a plaything for the masters, and she savored it. She couldn't resist taking a deep breath to inhale the scent of their commingled juices.

She was left drained and satisfied by both masters, and judging by the look of satisfaction and contentment on their faces, she had done the same to them.

Afterwards, Master James lapped lazily at her wet pussy, which she had thrust into his face as his back rested on the bed.

He had her ass cheeks in his firm hands, kneading, then pulling them wide apart so she felt the rush of air.

Master William, who was watching them closely, drooled as he approached the two, his eyes transfixed on the chocolate pot that peaked out between the black ass.

"There's still much more to learn," he said, his wet forefinger rubbing against the rim of her puckered rosebud. "Assuming, of course, that you want to."

"I do, Master James and Master William, I do."

The brothers looked at each other and smiled. It was the best birthday gift they'd ever had.

"Did I mention that we're just two of quadruplets?"

She gasped with surprise and her eyes opened wide at the possibilities.

TRIPLE PLEASURES

BWMW HISTORICAL SHORT

CHAPTER 1

*V*aneeta's life had taken an unexpected turn. She had been moved up from the grueling labor of the cotton fields to become a maid in the opulent main house.

This newfound role granted her a small room all to herself in a modest shack behind the main mansion.

The change in her circumstances was undeniable, and though not without its complexities, it was a step up from the hardships she had endured.

The small shack, though humble, was a sanctuary for Vaneeta. A space to call her own. It was nothing like the communal quarters she used to share with twenty other slaves in one room.

The solitude provided her with a semblance of privacy, a place where she could contemplate her desires and dreams away from prying eyes. Her Maw had been thankful.

She had always known her destiny and had accepted it a long time ago, but she probably did not know, or cared, about how much Vaneeta enjoyed being shared by the two masters.

The Bible did not support it, so she would be shocked.

Vaneeta, who worked as a maid in the main house, had a range of tasks to perform. Part of it was attending to the needs of the household, ensuring that the rooms were kept tidy and that the master and his guests were well-served.

She had the chance to observe the mansion's dynamics, thanks to the demanding role that required diligence and discretion.

Private parties with wanton women were held by visiting men while their wives slept close. Making sure they weren't discovered was part of her job.

Sometimes, she wished she could join in on the fun when she listened in. Once, she had seen one man with a marital aid shaped like a man's penis. It fascinated her because it was huge.

Her new status gave her some privileges and a bit of respect, but there was an underlying truth that clouded her newfound position.

Rumors circulated among the other slaves, whispers that Vaneeta had become the master's "plaything." It was a grim reality that many were aware of but chose not to speak about openly.

Vaneeta's heart weighed heavily with this knowledge, a reality she couldn't escape. The master's favoritism towards her was clear to all, and while it offered her protection and certain comforts, it came at a cost.

It was a reality she grappled with daily as she navigated the delicate balance between her desires and the limitations imposed upon her.

The master's gifts were both a source of pleasure and ambivalence for Vaneeta. The pretty things he bought her, the occasional new dress, and the attention he bestowed upon her created conflicting emotions within her.

She felt gratitude for the reprieve from the hardships of the cotton fields, yet the knowledge of the strings attached to these gifts lingered at the back of her mind. It didn't bother her. She loved being pleasured and giving pleasure to the master.

Vaneeta's fellow slaves observed her transformation, the envy mixed with understanding in their eyes. Her situation was complex, and they recognized the compromises she made to survive. Any of them would have done the same thing.

While some harbored a sense of resentment towards her new life, others extended empathy, knowing that survival often required navigating treacherous waters.

When Vaneeta left her bedroom in the main house and walked to the shed behind it, she felt every muscle and nerve in her body relax. It was there that she could reflect on her dreams.

The shack reeked of dirt and sweat, like poverty mixed with the scent of spices on the air from a distant kitchen. Her hands trailed over the rough timber wall, just as they had done many times before.

Part of her wanted to be a free slave, but part of her wanted to keep enjoying the addicting sex with her master and his twin when he visited.

When she pictured herself on top of them, fucking one

while fondling the other's balls as they tussled for control, she got wet.

She couldn't imagine it getting any better, but they had assured her it could when they fingered her asshole.

Master William was coming for a visit, and this time, he'd promised they would breach her asshole.

Was she ready? Surely, they would split her apart.

CHAPTER 2

The Masters had grown accustomed to their routine with Vaneeta, and although they looked forward to the occasional visit from other members of their family, they were always aware that time was fleeting and moments together should be cherished.

Master William was to return for his second visit in as many months, so addicted was he to the pleasures derived from the enslaved girl, he didn't mind the sacrifice of enduring the long journey.

The orgy ahead with his brother and Vaneeta would be a breath of fresh air, and no amount of trying to recreate it at his own plantation gave him the same pleasure.

The bout had invigorated both twins with fresh energy and passion. Master William envied the fact that Vaneeta was always there to cater to his brother's sexual desire.

As the day of Master William's arrival drew near, preparations were set in motion to receive him in a manner befitting his station. The mansion was meticulously cleaned; the gardens were groomed to perfection, and the kitchen was abuzz with culinary activity.

But this time, Master William's visit came with an unexpected twist. Just as he arrived, a telegram was delivered bearing unexpected news.

Master James read it with a furrowed brow before turning to his brother with a mix of surprise and concern.

"William, it seems that our other brother, Daniel, is on his way here for a visit," Master James announced, his voice laced with an unease that mirrored the sentiment in the room.

Daniel, the third quadruplet, was a name that invoked a range of emotions. Unlike his brothers, he had embraced a different path in life.

Time and money had transformed him into a figure that differed vastly from the memories his brothers held of him.

In contrast to Master James and Master William, who had maintained a sense of humanity despite their status, Daniel had ventured into the darker realms of slave trading and cotton sales.

He had amassed wealth, yes, but at a grave cost; losing empathy and compassion. His demeanor had shifted from pleasant to arrogant, his view of people tainted by the belief that they were mere possessions to be controlled.

As news of Daniel's impending arrival spread, a palpable tension settled over the plantation. The slaves, who had found solace in the presence of Master James and Master William, now feared this unknown figure whose reputation preceded him.

Was he here to buy slaves from his brother? Was he here to take over the plantation? Nobody knew, but they all feared something terrible because there would be three masters, something that had never happened before.

What did it all mean?

The day finally when Master Daniel stepped foot on the plantation. Dressed in lavish attire that exuded wealth, he appeared almost like a stranger to his own family.

His eyes held a coldness, a detachment that sent shivers down the spines of those who crossed his path.

Vaneeta watched from a distance as the three brothers conversed. She had been warned to stay far away from the new master.

Masters James and William maintained a sense of decorum, but their expressions masked their discomfort. Master Daniel, however, carried an air of superiority that was hard to ignore.

A feeling of unease settled over the plantation as the evening approached. The slaves heard tales of Master Daniel's cruel nature from the entourage he had brought with him.

Some bore marks from the whippings they had received at his hands.

According to their reports, he had a preference for using a whip with blades to cause wounds that would have a lasting effect.

He treated people as mere commodities, and their fears were validated as they witnessed his interactions firsthand.

He was dismissive and cold, referring to the slaves as if

they were invisible entities. His arrogance permeated the air, leaving a bitter taste of disdain for those beneath him.

Isabella's heart sank as she observed his interactions, her hopes being with the two masters dimming in the presence of such brutality.

They couldn't risk being seen with a slave by their brother. With any luck, she prayed he would leave soon.

Under the shade of the ancient trees that had witnessed generations come and go, a lavish spread was laid out in picnic style.

Tables were adorned with checkered cloths, and platters overflowed with mouthwatering dishes like fried chicken, sweet potato pie, and cornbread. Vaneeta watched from afar.

Master Daniel, the third quadruplet, was a commanding presence at the luncheon. Dressed in attire that exuded wealth and power, he carried himself with an air of arrogance that was impossible to ignore.

His interactions were laced with condescension, his gaze sweeping over the gathered guests with a sense of entitlement.

Afterwards, Master Daniel retired to the mansion, his arrogance and cruelty leaving a lingering discomfort in his wake.

The plantation, once a place of varying emotions, was now consumed by the specter of a new presence.

Master Daniel, a man who viewed humanity through a lens of ownership and power, had cast an ominous shadow.

It seemed to Vaneeta that the other two masters feared their brother. That made her fearful, too.

CHAPTER 3

*V*aneeta was restless. She had been told to stay away from Master Daniel, but she was fascinated by him.

How could someone who was a carbon copy of his brothers be so different?

Without thinking, she made her way to the mansion to get a slice of leftover pie because her stomach was rumbling.

She walked softly past the room where Master Daniel slept, but he heard the footsteps anyway and called out in a loud voice for the person to enter.

Terrified and excited at the same time, she opened the door and peered inside. There, in the room, was master Daniel fucking one maid who was bent over on the giant oak desk.

While looking up at her, he asked her to bring him some lemonade without stopping his thrusting deep into the girl.

The white maid looked bored but resigned as she whimpered with groans of mock pleasure.

Vaneeta glanced at his arm muscles and saw that he had a twisted smile on his face when he plunged into the young woman, who gasped each time he drove into her.

The machine-like rhythm turned Vaneeta on and made her long to feel his cock inside her body. His cock, she observed, looked chubbier than his other brothers.

Her pussy got wet as she was rooted to the spot. The look of lust was in his eyes ran over her body and she felt naked even though she was covered from head to toe.

A voice outside brought her back to her senses, and she stepped out quickly to fetch the lemonade, her legs trembling as she moved.

She didn't waste any time returning with the lemonade, as she didn't want to get into trouble.

The same gruff voice of before told her to come in after she knocked. She walked in with caution as she wondered if he was still pounding into the girl.

However, he was done with the maid and her ass was covered with his cum. He was jabbing two fingers in and out of her cunny, then pulled out and stuffed them in the girl's mouth.

"Taste yourself," he said with pride, and she did. Master Daniel had not bothered to cover himself and his cock jutted out from his body, thick, slimy, and wet.

He motioned for the cup, and she advanced towards him with trepidation.

As he took the cup from her with one hand, the other hand suddenly fondled her breast.

She didn't flinch as he rubbed and pulled at a nipple

which was already hardened. His cock got stiffer, and she was glad of the effect she had on him.

A voice then came from outside the room. "Daniel, are you in there?" She recognized Master James' voice.

Had he come to save her once again?

The only problem was that she wasn't sure she wanted to be saved.

Indeed, Master James was there to claim his slave. After being alerted as to Vaneeta's whereabouts, he had walked, and almost run into the mansion with his brother right behind him.

Neither one wanted him to flog Vaneeta and damage her beautiful skin.

CHAPTER 4

There was some unspoken communication between the three brothers after Masters' James and William opened the door to find a naked Daniel fondling Vaneeta.

In the end, Master Daniel gave a slight nod to his brothers, but she was not privy to it.

Vaneeta trembled as she heard Mr Daniel's commanding tone telling her to strip naked so he could see what she offered.

She removed her clothes as her mind raced until she was completely naked.

Master Daniel and the two brothers seemed to enjoy the sight of her exposed body, and a wave of pleasure swept through her body with their gazes firmly on her.

She then stood before them, her beautiful dark chocolate skin on full display and her nipples stiff from the excitement.

Mr James suddenly spoke up, delivering orders he had

in mind for Vaneeta. "Since Daniel is our guest, we should let him decide first."

Master William nodded his agreement, his cock at attention as he drooled.

Master Daniel commanded her to kneel between the two brothers and kiss them both. She obeyed, pressing her lips against each of the brothers in turn as they both groaned in pleasure at the intimate feeling.

He had always thought the slaves were inferior, but looking at his brothers' faces and seeing their enjoyment, he was conflicted.

They didn't have a problem with sharing saliva with a slave. In fact, the opposite was true.

His cock got stronger as he watched, and he longed to fuck her black pussy without haste. The wet, pinkish vulva enticed him as her ass danced before his eyes.

Once throughly aroused and felt he would explode, Master Daniel chose her pussy to fuck first.

He descended upon her, pushing her thighs wide, exposing all of her loins, and plunged without preamble.

If he had hoped to split her wide open, it didn't happen because Vaneeta's pussy was already slick with her own juices and he was received with little difficulty.

The brothers rushed to lay claim on their share. James, happy that his brother had not claimed what he feverishly wanted for himself, taunted her asshole with his tongue, widening it with his fingers in anticipation of fucking it for the first time.

Master William drove his cock in and out of her mouth, his balls banging against her throat.

Vaneeta was experiencing heavenly sensations as every part of her body was involved.

But this was only the beginning of her sexual journey with the triplets. Vaneeta was pulled onto Master William's lap after a brief break for refreshments.

His stubby, rough fingers plied open her wet cunt and burrowed deep into her loins till his cock was buried tot he hilt.

He licked his fingers and rubbed at her pussy while she rose and fell on his weapon. Her head was thrown back, and she moaned loudly as she thrashed. He was fascinated by the sight of her breasts swaying before him.

Vaneeta's pussy was stretched to the limit as she rode Master William's pego. Master Daniel once again stood, keeping watch as his brothers pleasured her.

She stared as he tugged at his manhood and watched as it grew before her eyes.

Master James appeared out of nowhere then and bent her over his brother's body. Once again, he licked her asshole, sometimes sliding a wet finger in it. The sensation was spine tingling, and she pushed back against his mouth.

"Are you ready, Vaneeta?"

The scent of her skin drove him wild, and he kissed across her back and shoulders as his hands traveled down her body.

His cock sought his destination; her ass, and he reveled knowing that he was the first to drill into her secret cave.

His fingers toiled their way around, slowly exploring

the tight, puckered hole in anticipation of what was to come.

With a single deep breath, he spread her ass cheeks wide, and pressed the knob of his cock against her entrance.

Vaneeta's eyes widened in surprise as she let out a gasp. Before she could utter a protest, he pressed onward with a steady, unrelenting force.

Her howl of pain and pleasure intoxicated him, and he grinned with delight as he felt her body relax around him.

He moved, slowly and gently at first, coaxing her to accept him as her pleasure mounted.

"Act like you're going to void, and that'll make that ripe asshole open for my steed."

"You're doing just fine, girl. We're so darn proud of you," encouraged Master William.

With each thrust, her body moved in time with his, arching to meet him, and he became lost in the throes of their passion.

He felt her walls quiver and knew that she was close to climaxing, so he increased his intensity, pushing her to the brink of bliss so they could reach the peak together.

Once Vaneeta got used to the invasion, she loved the sensation of feeling both brothers in her entrails.

CHAPTER 5

$\mathcal{V}$aneeta could feel her insides invaded by both brothers and she felt the thin veil that separated master James in her ass and master William in her pussy.

The initial pain had now deemed and only pleasure remained as both brothers fucked her at seemingly the same pace.

She moaned and screamed with each thrust, their cocks filling her up completely, pushing against each other as they moved in tandem.

Vaneeta was lost in a haze of pleasure, and felt as if her body didn't belong to her anymore, but to these two powerful men who were taking complete control of it.

The sensation was intense, each stroke sending waves of pleasure through her body as they pushed further into her depths. She felt herself reaching new heights of pleasure with every second that passed.

The force of the two men inside her at the same time

overwhelmed with sensations foreign. This was the first time they had defiled her butthole. Before now, she had only known it to serve one function.

Her breath quickened as she felt an orgasm building up within her. She looked up pleadingly into Master Daniel's eyes, surprising him with her request to join them. He moved closer to the bed, his hard cock throbbing in anticipation.

Without hesitation, he grasped Vaneeta's hair from behind and pushed himself into her mouth.

His thrusts were powerful yet gentle, eliciting deep moans from Vaneeta that reverberated through the room.

His hands roamed over her body as he intensified his movements, pushing all three lovers closer to the edge of release.

The sensation of being fucked by all three brothers at the same time drove her mad with pleasure.

She felt them all deeply, their thrusts and movements synchronized in perfect harmony as they brought her to new heights of pleasure.

Master James' thick cock pushing deep into her ass as his thrusts grew deeper and faster.

Master William's steady rhythm driving him deep inside her essence. And Master Daniel's massive weapon servicing her oral cavity left her screaming for more.

Vaneeta was on the brink of ecstasy when she felt something strange - a warmth emanating from within her body that increased with every thrust, radiating outwards until it seemed to fill the entire room.

With one last roar, she reached her climax, and it was

like a wave crashing over her soul, gifting them all with an intense pleasure that none of them had experienced before.

THE INTENSITY of their lovemaking built until it reached a crescendo of thundering pleasure.

CHAPTER 6

The brothers continued to take turns at Vaneeta's body throughout the night. Master James was always first, eagerly filling her tight hole with his cock.

Then came Master William, who pushed in deeply between her wet lips, making her moan with pleasure.

Then again, it was Master Daniel who took his place, pushing past her lips and filling her mouth with his manhood. Vaneeta was pulled in many directions as all three brothers pleasured her, each in their own way.

They moved around the room, taking turns at all her openings. Sometimes she would be on her knees other and times she would be arched over them.

Back and forth, they shared control and enjoyed every second. Even when they switched from one to another, she never felt neglected, as each brother had their own unique way of making her feel pleasure, and that kept Vaneeta wanting more.

Master Daniel had an intense way of looking at Vanetta. His eyes seemed to pierce her soul, making her lay bare before him.

His thick, long cock stretched her tight asshole to the limits and even though it was a bit more painful for Vanetta, she loved the sensation of being filled up with his enormous cock.

The brothers took turns ramming in and out of her tight hole as they brought her to the brink of orgasm multiple times.

Vanetta felt as though she was living in a dream world as all three brothers steadily pounded away at her body from different angles simultaneously.

They caressed and kissed her body in between thrusts and each time they switched places, she could feel them stretching out every single inch of her inner walls until there was nothing left of her untouched.

At one point, Master William opened her wet pussy lips wide and inhaled deeply, smelling the mixture of her juice, his and his brothers. He lapped at her sweet nectarine with his tongue, sending shivers throughout her body.

He raced from one side to the other, tantalizingly slowly. His tongue moved like a snake exploring all the hidden crevices before diving inside her asshole as well.

With slow circular motions, he explored until she felt his whole tongue teasing her insides. Master William's actions were so arousing that Vaneeta moved rhythmically against him as he explored deeper and deeper inside her.

Master James took over and pushed both brothers aside to take advantage of the pleasure she was offering. His gigantic hands cupped both of her buttocks while he started thrusting deep inside her pussy, each thrust faster than the last one, bringing them closer and closer to complete ecstasy.

By now Vaneeta was panting heavily; she could barely take all three brothers at once, but as soon as they reached their climax, she screamed in pleasure as well.

The sensation of all three men coming together was almost too much for her because who lay in a puddle of bliss afterwards, completely spent of energy but full of satisfaction.

Vanetta felt completely ravished by this point and just when she thought it couldn't get any better, Master Daniel drove himself into her one last time and released a powerful stream of cum deep inside her belly. Indeed, that famous session with the three brothers would stay with Vanetta for the rest of eternity!

The brothers stayed on top of her for some minutes more, gently caressing her body before finally allowing themselves to slide off from Vaneeta's exhausted body.

She lay there feeling every inch of pleasure they had provided until finally drifting off into a satisfied sleep while all three brothers stood by admiring their work.

The night seemed to go on forever, until finally, they all finished within seconds of each other and collapsed into a heaping pile of bodies.

Vaneeta lay still, trying to catch her breath, and the brothers lay beside her in blissful exhaustion.

She looked into Master Daniel's eyes and saw only

adoration there for the woman who had just given them so much pleasure.

With a triumphant sigh, she settled into the embrace of all three brothers, safely knowing that she belonged only to them now.

CHAPTER 7

The days following the grand luncheon witnessed an unexpected transformation in Master Daniel.

The same man who had arrived at the plantation with an air of arrogance and dismissiveness now displayed a demeanor that was markedly different.

It was as if the experience had left a mark on him, altering his perspective in ways that surprised those who saw him.

That change was felt by everyone, from his staff to the slaves who toiled on the plantation.

His interactions were characterized by a gentler tone, a kinder approach that seemed to emanate from a place of newfound understanding.

The once-gruff master now displayed a willingness to listen, a willingness to acknowledge the humanity of those around him.

The slaves noticed the shift immediately. They exchanged glances of both surprise and cautious hope, unsure of whether this change was merely temporary or the result of a genuine shift in his outlook.

Whispers spread through the quarters, tales of small kindnesses and moments of consideration that were unusual coming from Master Daniel.

Vaneeta, who had silently observed the events unfold, found herself caught between skepticism and a sliver of optimism.

Could it be that her contribution to his wanton pleasure had somehow contributed to this change? It was a thought she dared not voice, yet it lingered in her mind.

The next two days brought further evidence of this transformation. Master Daniel seemed genuinely happier.

The slaves worked diligently under the warm sun, heartened by the subtle changes they observed.

There was a shared sense of curiosity, a cautious optimism that perhaps this was the beginning of a new era. Though there were rumours of war and mutiny, it had not yet affected them. Still, they knew acutely that the path towards change was fraught with uncertainty.

The older slaves that worked in the mansion knew about his trysts with his other two brothers and Vaneeta, and suspected that was the root of it all. They'd heard the noises of the orgies.

On the third day, upon his departure, Master Daniel approached his brother, Mr. James, with a request.

They stood in the shade of the old trees, their voices hushed as they engaged in a conversation that held the potential to reshape their family dynamics.

"I have been reflecting on my time here," Master

Daniel began, his tone earnest, "and I am struck by the impact this place has had on me."

Mr. James regarded his brother with a mix of curiosity and caution. "You seem changed, Daniel. The difference in your demeanor is striking."

A sigh escaped Master Daniel's lips as he nodded. "It's as if a veil has been lifted from my eyes. I see things differently now, James. I understand the weight of responsibility that comes with the privileges we have."

He paused, his gaze distant as he continued, "I have been thinking, perhaps it is time for us to bridge the gap between our brothers."

Mr. James's brow furrowed slightly in surprise. "You mean you want to bring our fourth brother into the fold?" They both knew he was talking about Vaneeta.

A pensive expression settled over Master Daniel's face. "Yes. We have been separated for far too long. Our parents' deaths cast a shadow over our relationship, but I believe that time and experience have given us the chance to mend what was broken."

Mr. James considered his brother's words, no hint of conviction in his eyes. "It won't be easy, Daniel. He has changed as well, shaped by his own experiences."

Master Daniel nodded, a sense of determination in his gaze. "I understand that, James. But I believe we owe it to ourselves and our parents' memory to at least try."

A contemplative silence settled between the brothers, the weight of their history and the potential for reconciliation hanging in the air.

Vaneeta, who had discreetly observed the conversation from a distance, couldn't help but feel a sense of awe at the power of transformation. She also knew that her sexual prowess was powerful.

As the brothers continued their conversation, discussing plans and possibilities, Vaneeta's heart swelled with a mix of emotions.

The transformation she had witnessed in Master Daniel was a testament to the power of her black pussy.

Perhaps, just perhaps, this glimmer of hope could extend beyond the plantation, beyond the confines of their world, and pave the way for a future where people were not only free slaves, but sexually free too and could love whomever they chose.

If the fourth master joined them, would he also succumb to the sinful sexual pleasure?

AUTHOR'S NOTE

Thank you for your purchase. You can sign up to my mailing list to receive notification whenever a new book releases.

If you enjoyed it, I would appreciate a customer review on whatever platform you purchased it from.

Join here: or scan with your phone:

QUADRUPLE PLEASURES

BWWM HISTORICAL SHORT - PLANTATION TALES 3

CHAPTER 1

The serene atmosphere that surrounded the grand old plantation was unlike anything seen before, because it created a sense of peace and tranquility.

Gentle rustling leaves from the grand old trees filled the air, and the fields stood still, a stark contrast to the usual bustle of labor. It was a time of serenity, more than the usual and the whispers of hope lingered like a gentle breeze.

Most of the slaves had noticed it, and more than one thought it was because of the happiness of the master, especially when his brothers visited.

Vaneeta was responsible for much of this but they all enjoyed the fruits of her labor.

It was assumed by them she exerted her influence over him, leading to the possibility that he had instructed the handlers, as there appeared to be a decrease in using the switch and even occasional displays of humane reactions from them.

During this calm, Vaneeta moved through the main

house with a certain grace that came with her newfound status.

Her days were filled with tasks that befit her role as a maid that served only the master, and the privileges that came with it were clear.

Her mother, once toiling under the harsh sun in the cotton fields, now found refuge in the slave quarters, spared from the relentless labor that had defined her existence.

She had refused to move in with Vaneeta because she wanted the master to come and go without her being in the way.

It would be incorrect to label her as ignorant because she knew exactly what her daughter was doing with the master.

The happenings in the mansion, in relation to her daughter, were not something she felt inclined to pass judgment on. Had she been in the same position, she would have undoubtedly made the same decision.

The focus of her life experience was centered on survival, and she felt a deep sense of satisfaction knowing that she had brought into the world a stunning young woman who captivated the hearts of men.

The difference between the tranquility of the main house and the remnants of hardship in the slave quarters was a constant reminder of their lot in life.

Vaneeta carried herself with a quiet dignity, mindful of the struggles that persisted beyond the privileged realms she now occupied. The other slaves no longer looked at her with scorn or judgement in their eyes.

However, even though everything seemed peaceful, there was still an underlying sense of anticipation.

The invitation extended by the three brothers to their estranged sibling hung in the air like a question mark. The decision to make peace was an unusual one, especially considering the strained history between them.

Vaneeta speculated on the cause behind this gesture, although she already had a notion of the expected outcome. Each of the four brothers would have a share of her. Would she be able to satisfy all of them?

Meanwhile, two states away, the fourth brother, Adam, received the unexpected invitation. His initial reaction was one of suspicion.

He had never been the favored brother, always an outsider in the familial dynamics. The brothers' sudden desire for reconciliation struck him as odd, and he couldn't shake the feeling that there was a catch.

He would go to the extent of saying that they despised him, that's how strongly he felt their dislike towards him.

His life had taken a different path. He had built his own fortune besides the one left by their parents, one that had distanced him from the ties of kinship.

This happened after he'd involved himself with a secret society who traded opium, something his brothers had frowned upon.

The scars of past resentments lingered, and he questioned the sincerity behind the invitation.

Yet, curiosity gnawed at him. What could his brothers want now? Why extend an olive branch after all these years?

After careful consideration, he agreed to meet them.

The journey to the plantation was a blend of reluctance and intrigue.

The memories of childhood, marked by competition and animosity, resurfaced. He couldn't deny the complexity of the emotions that swirled within him.

Back at the plantation, a messenger was dispatched to convey the acceptance of the invitation. The brothers awaited his arrival with a mix of hope and nervousness.

Vaneeta sensed a shift in the air. The peaceful stillness that had settled over the estate was now burdened by the lingering tales of unresolved pasts and the ambiguous hope for a future that hung in the balance between redemption and further discord.

The way she perceived it, the brothers were filled with fear in anticipation of the visitor who was about to arrive.

Was he cruel to his own flesh and blood? If that was true, how would he be with the slaves?

CHAPTER 2

*I*n the plantation's heart, Vaneeta's mother, once a weary laborer in the cotton fields, now found herself in a position that carried a different weight.

With unwavering dedication, she tirelessly toiled away in the spacious kitchen of the grand main house, diligently making sure that every meal served showcased the rich culinary heritage deeply rooted in the fertile southern soil.

The kitchen had become a shelter and filled with fragrant spices and simmering stews.

The clinking of utensils and the rhythmic chopping of vegetables were music that echoed through the corridors of the main house.

Vaneeta's mother, with a newfound sense of purpose, took pride in her role. She had witnessed the transformation of her daughter's life, and it was her turn to contribute to the changing dynamics of the plantation.

Vaneeta, now entrusted with the duties of a maid, found solace in the comforting aromas that wafted from the kitchen. Her mother, ever watchful and protective, made sure that Vaneeta was well-fed.

It was a minor act of defiance against the hardships they had endured, a subtle assertion of dignity in the face of inequality.

Vaneeta's curiosity about the impending arrival of the fourth brother, the elusive figure in the quadruplet, had grown like a quiet flame in her heart. She couldn't deny the trepidation that accompanied her thoughts.

The reputation that preceded him painted a picture of strength and authority, characteristics that, in her world, could dictate the course of her fate.

Yet, amidst the worry, there lingered a quiet confidence. Vaneeta was aware of the allure she held, the womanly charms that had, in part, elevated her status within the main house.

She had observed the brothers' kindness, their willingness to extend certain privileges. There was a silent understanding that, perhaps, her position held a delicate balance of power. Maybe that would extend to the fourth brother.

As she moved through her daily tasks, anticipation mingled with anxiety the closer the time came for the arrival. The prospect of meeting the fourth brother brought a flurry of emotions.

She wondered about the man behind the reputation, the complexities that had shaped his life. It was a constant change between fear and curiosity, a delicate dance that mirrored the rhythms of the plantation itself.

In the evenings when the sun set, Vaneeta would steal moments of solitude by the kitchen window. She loved the smells of the kitchen and she also enjoyed being near the master, just in case he wanted her.

Sometimes she had a fear that he would find another slave to enjoy and send her back to the slave quarters. It was a feeling she couldn't entirely shake, even though there had been no sign of that.

The night before the fourth brother's arrival, Vaneeta's mother approached her with a knowing smile. "Child, the winds of change are blowing through this plantation," she remarked, her eyes reflecting a quiet wisdom.

Vaneeta nodded, her gaze fixed on the blowing wind outside.

"I can feel it, Mama. There's something stirring, and I don't know whether to be afraid or hopeful."

Her mother's hands, weathered from years of labor, cupped Vaneeta's face with a tenderness that spoke of a mother's love and resilience.

"You are stronger than you know, Vaneeta. The strength of a woman is not always in the muscles, but in the heart. Remember that, no matter what comes."

As the night unfolded, Vaneeta pondered her mother's words. The fragrance of change hung in the air, a scent that carried both the sweetness of possibility and the bitterness of the unknown.

The fourth brother would mark a new chapter in her story, and Vaneeta prepared to face the winds of change that whispered through the moonlit fields.

CHAPTER 3

As the carriage came to a halt before the grand entrance of the main house, the rays of the morning sun covered the plantation in tranquil shades of gold and amber.

The fourth master, Adam, marked a momentous occasion — the reunion of the estranged quadruplets.

As he stepped out, the similarities with his brothers were striking, yet a subtle distinction set him apart. His beard. It was bushy and framed a face that bore a demeanor of suspicion.

His eyes, sharp and perceptive, scanned his surroundings with a wariness that hinted at a lifetime of guarded experiences.

Dressed in attire that echoed the wealth and stature befitting a plantation owner, Adam carried himself with a quiet authority.

The brothers, awaiting him on the porch, greeted him with a mix of familiarity and formality.

Adam's gaze fell upon his brothers, their features a

reflection of shared lineage.

It was a moment suspended in time, a reunion that held the weight of years gone by. The air crackled with unspoken tensions, the ghosts of childhood grievances lingering like shadows.

As the brothers exchanged pleasantries, Vaneeta observed from a discreet distance hidden behind an old oak tree, her eyes tracing the contours of this unfamiliar figure in the plantation's narrative.

She noted the suspicion in his gaze, the guarded nature that seemed to shield him from the vulnerability of familial ties. There was someone with him.

Standing beside Adam was a young woman, her dark skin embellished with the beautiful richness that only the sun's warm embrace could provide.

Her afro, a crown of unapologetic beauty, framed a face that spoke of resilience. The curves of her body, emphasized by a silhouette that bore the hallmarks of a unique beauty, set her apart from Vaneeta.

Master Adam was ushered into a suite in the mansion, a space befitting his status as a member of the family.

The new slave girl, with a hesitance in her step, was informed that she would share quarters with Vaneeta.

Her eyes betrayed a mixture of perception and curiosity, a reflection of the uncertainty that marked her arrival.

Vaneeta ran back to her quarters as soon as she heard them, so she'd be there to welcome the girl. A few seconds after she got in, there was a knock, followed by the entrance of the new girl.

The contrast between the two young women was quite apparent. Vaneeta, with her refined elegance, and the new slave girl, with a beauty that impressed with a different rhythm, faced each other in a moment that held the potential for camaraderie or discord.

Vaneeta, sensing the apprehension in her new companion, extended a warm smile. "Welcome," she said, her voice a soothing melody. "There's no need to worry. You're safe here."

With a desperate longing for reassurance, the new slave girl's eyes anxiously scanned Vaneeta's face. "I don't understand why we're here. Do you know? Are they planning to sell us?"

Vaneeta's gaze softened with empathy. "No, no. There's no talk of selling. They're family, the brothers. I think they just want to be a family again."

The relief that washed over the new slave girl's face was noticeable. The withheld tension melted away from her shoulders and a hesitant smile slowly appeared on her lips in its place.

With a graceful gesture, Vaneeta extended her hand, indicating her desire to establish a friendship.

As time passed, the room, once a symbol of uncertainty, underwent a transformation and became a space where connections took shape as the girls shared their experiences of slave life.

Meanwhile, in the mansion's grandeur, the four brothers engaged in conversations that about their shared memories.

In order to maintain a positive atmosphere, the three intentionally avoided bringing up the unsavory business that Adam was a part of. He knew how they felt and there was no use reopening old wounds.

The sincerity behind their invitation gradually became apparent to Adam, causing his suspicion to soften as time went by.

Despite being mindful of the wounds of the past, they were slowly being overshadowed by the hope of reconciliation.

As the day unfolded, the plantation echoed with the footsteps of a newfound kinship.

The winds of reckoning, set in motion by the fourth master, carried with them the promise of change, one that, perhaps, held the key to healing the fractures of a family divided by time and circumstance.

CHAPTER 4

The next day, after Adam had settled in, the atmosphere in the mansion shifted as the brothers gathered in the study.

Master Adam, his eyes still carrying the suspicion of a guarded past, stood with a certain possessiveness beside his slave girl.

Even though she was dressed in simple clothing, her striking beauty had not gone unnoticed by the other brothers. Adam introduced them to her, although he was not enthusiastic about it. That was clear to see for most.

As they exchanged stories and plans for the days ahead, one brother, oblivious to the undercurrents, remarked on the striking beauty of Master Adam's slave girl.

The words hung in the air, a momentary pause that shattered the illusion of unity.

Master Adam's demeanor hardened instantly, a possessive glint in his eyes. "She's mine. Exclusive. Keep away from her," he declared, his tone leaving no room for negotiation.

The brothers exchanged uneasy glances. Their attempts to understand the paradox of Master Adam's possessiveness met with confusion.

If she was indeed his exclusive property, why did he treat her with a detached coldness, as if she were a mere object?

In a fit of frustration, Master Adam stormed off, his parting words a declaration of his perceived entitlement. "I can do whatever I like."

The remaining brothers shook their heads in unison. It seemed, in that moment, that some things hadn't changed at all. The shadows of past disputes, it appeared, still cast their influence over the present.

Their brother's behavior remained unchanged, as he continued to be a boor and a bully, showing no regard for anyone besides himself.

After carefully discussing and considering the best approach to handle this delicate situation, a final decision was reached.

There would be an intimate dinner of the four brothers and the two slave girls, a gathering that would serve as a gesture of goodwill and an attempt to smooth the rough edges of familial discord.

The following evening, the main hall of the mansion was transformed into a haven of decadence. Soft candlelight flickered, casting a warm glow over the gathering.

Intricate table settings adorned with silverware and fine china awaited the guests, and the air was filled with the alluring scent of exotic flowers handpicked by Vaneeta's mother.

The theme of the event revolved around decadence, which was a lavish celebration of opulence and indulgence.

An entertainer, a maestro of song and dance, had been enlisted to entertain them with melodies that would serve as both distraction and enchantment.

After Master Adam with his slave girl, the decadent affair unfolded as the three brothers preceded him.

The evening was punctuated by laughter, the clinking of glasses, and the melodies that filled the air.

The entertainer's performance captivated the small audience and eased the tension of the day before.

Master Adam, despite his initial reservations, found himself drawn into the charm of the evening. The hypnotizing performance seemed to soften the rigid lines of possessiveness that marked his demeanor.

For a moment, the weight of the past seemed to lift, and the brothers, despite their differences, shared a space where the strains of discord were replaced by the harmony of shared memories.

Their parents used to hold such intimate affairs and as little kids, they would watch from the top of the stairs of the mansion.

As the night wore on, the decadent feast and the alcoholic consumption became a balm for the wounds of estrangement.

The brothers, in their shared pursuit of reconciliation, allowed themselves to be carried away by the rhythms of the evening, and call a truce for the night.

CHAPTER 5

The air in the Vaneeta's quarters hummed with anticipation as she stood before her small, weathered mirror.

The outfit she wore was a displayed the artistry of a skilled seamstress, which in this case, was her mother, who had a creation that blended elegance with the modesty befitting the era.

Her figure was beautifully highlighted by the fabric, a stunning hue of indigo, which stressed her grace and femininity.

The delicate lace along the neckline added a touch of refinement, and the hem grazed the floor as she twirled, the skirt swirling around her like a cascade of midnight stars.

Vaneeta felt empowered in that moment because the elegant fabric shielded her from the harsh realities of her life. She felt like a human being that wasn't defined by her color.

Across the room, the other slave girl, Naima, still

unaccustomed to such displays of care, hesitated before the dreary outfit she had worn countless times.

To her surprise, she discovered a second garment draped over her simple cot. The fabric was a muted lavender, adorned with modest embroidery that hinted at a quiet style.

Vaneeta, noticing the hesitation, approached with a warm smile. "Looks like the brothers wanted you to shine tonight, too. Go on, try it. You deserve to feel beautiful."

As the new slave girl slipped into the unexpected gift, her reflection in the mirror revealed a transformation.

The lavender fabric embraced her curves with a newfound elegance. The embroidery, a delicate touch against her skin, spoke of the effort put into choosing an outfit that transcended the ordinary.

The two girls shared a moment of quiet gratitude. The unspoken acknowledgment of the kindness extended to them touched a chord that resonated beyond the constraints of their circumstances.

The preparation for the grand affair took time — every button, every fold, every strand of hair meticulously attended to.

Vaneeta and the new slave girl, Naima, united by the shared experience of being seen as more than mere possessions, reveled in this opportunity to adorn themselves in the threads of dignity.

As they entered the main hall, the gasps of admiration that greeted them were almost palpable.

The dark hues of the gentlemen's outfits provided a striking scenery for the contrasting yet harmonious indigo and lavender hues, making them stand out even more.

Master Adam, standing across the room, observed his slave girl with fresh eyes. The unfamiliar garments transformed her, revealing a beauty he had overlooked in the familiarity of the every day. He felt ashamed that his brothers had done something he hadn't thought of doing.

However, the realization that not only he, but also his brothers found her newfound allure captivating, ignited a possessiveness consumed him, one that he simply couldn't overlook.

In a tone that cut through the festive atmosphere, Master Adam ordered his slave girl to return to her room. The tension in the room shot up.

There was a hushed expectancy, as the girl hesitated. It was a moment that held the weight of defiance, the first act of resistance against the chains of ownership. A moment she would remember for the rest of her life.

"I want to stay," she declared, her voice steady. The three brothers exchanged glances and they were secretly pleased. They had plans for her.

With a grunt of reluctant acknowledgment because he didn't want to lose face, Master Adam conceded, acknowledging the request.

The girls remained, their presence a subtle rebellion against the traditional power dynamics that governed their lives.

As the night unfolded, Naima's confidence grew as she took the lead from Vaneeta who took turns sitting on the laps of the three masters while the other girl stayed with master Adam.

The boundaries of tradition were gently pushed aside for the evening and the slave girls were all that mattered.

Even in a world defined by ownership, the spirit could transcend the limitations imposed upon it and they were living proof of that.

CHAPTER 6

Naima and Vaneeta were to be the sexual entertainment of the night once dinner was done with and the music entertainer left.

They moved the party to one of the bedrooms in the mansion. This was to be a night of debauchery.

Adam turned to his brothers with a smirk on his face and announced, "Tonight, my dear brothers, Naima is mine only."

His brothers looked at him with disappointment. Naima at first, had felt a little uneasy at the thought of being watched while she was intimate with her master and had mentioned it to Vaneeta, but she was encouraged by Vaneeta's words.

"Considering how much the brothers look alike, just picture four of your master. It will quadruple your pleasure," she said knowingly.

The brothers nodded their agreement but couldn't hide their disappointment.

They had been looking forward to having some lecherous fun with the beautiful slave, in addition to their own adventurous beauty.

Vaneeta then eagerly responded to the request of master Daniel by shedding her clothes slowly, taking time to rub her nipples which were already stiff.

She bent over as she took off her stockings which were damp from her pussy juice.

From between her legs spread far apart, she spied all four men looking at her with the bulges of their cocks evident as each stroked their member.

She smiled because master Adam, even though he was kneading Naima's full breasts, was staring slack jawed at her pussy.

He desired to fuck her too and it gave her a sense of power over him. To have her, he would surely have to let Naima in on the excitement. She knew the other brothers would insist on that.

Once Vaneeta was fully devoid of clothing, master Daniel motioned for her to join him on the bed where he was already laying, his cock stiff and oozing pre-cum.

She crawled towards him seductively, swaying her hips in a sensual manner that made the brothers' groins ache with desire.

Naima watched from the side as master Daniel ravished Vaneeta, his hands roaming all over her body as he kissed and nipped at her skin. She saw that Vaneeta was enjoying every moment of it, moaning and gasping under his touch.

Unable to resist any longer, master Adam let go of Naima's breasts and approached Vaneeta from behind.

He began to kiss and caress her back while master Daniel focused on her breasts and pussy.

Naima felt a surge of arousal at the sight before her that was unlike anything she had ever felt and her hand dropped to cup her own mound which was already moist.

The brothers were now taking turns pleasuring Vaneeta's body, their hands exploring every inch of her as they worshipped her like a goddess.

Feeling left out, Naima approached them slowly. She wanted to join in on the action.

She crawled towards the bed and took one of Vaneeta's nipples into her mouth, sucking on it while she ran her hand down Vaneeta's stomach towards where master Daniel was thrusting into her.

As she watched Vaneeta's body writhe beneath the muscular man on top of her, she felt the heat between her legs.

Her finger traced along the slick folds of her own sex as she fantasized about being in Vaneeta's place, with that immense cock plunging into her over and over again. She couldn't resist rubbing herself, feeling her arousal grow with each stroke.

Vaneeta moaned as master Adam's lips closed around her other nipple, sucking and nibbling on it while his hand cupped her breast. She arched her back, pressing herself closer to him as she felt an erection against her thigh.

Master Daniel continued to thrust into her with a steady rhythm, his cock hitting all the right spots inside of her. She could feel her orgasm building, spurred on by the dual stimulation from both brothers and Naima.

When Vaneeta felt Naima's softer hands on her body, the new sensation sent her over the edge and she screamed out into the void with pleasure and spurted her juice around master Daniel's cock.

As she lay panting on the bed, master Adam went and took his place between Naima's legs. He spread them wide apart before licking and sucking at her wet pussy eagerly.

He used his stubby fingers to spread open Naima's folds and expertly swallowed every drop of her pungent juice it was driving him close to the edge.

It was one thing when they were alone, but to have his brothers and Vaneeta watching was like an aphrodisiac.

Naima moaned loudly as pleasure coursed through her body. She couldn't believe how amazing all of it felt.

She felt one of the brothers push his erect member into the mouth and it caught her by surprise, almost gagging her but she recovered quickly, sucking with all her might.

Vaneeta watched from the side with a smirk on her face as Naima squirmed under the brothers' talented tongues and cocks. She joined in, this time taking master Daniel's cock in hand and stroking him as he pleasured Naima.

The room was filled with moans and gasps as they all reached their peaks together. Master Adam sucked harder on Naima's clit while master Daniel thrust into Vaneeta's hand one final time before releasing himself in hot spurts all over her fingers.

Naima's body shook with the intensity of her orgasm as she felt the brothers' cum splash across her thighs.

Vaneeta watched with a mix of satisfaction and envy,

knowing that she had helped herself and the others achieve such pleasure.

Their sexual activities continued, each one taking turns pleasuring the others in a variety of ways. The mansion echoed with their cries of passion and the sound of bodies slapping against one another. There was no one to hear them.

One by one, they finished their sessions, collapsing onto the bed in a heap of sweaty, satiated bodies. Naima, Vaneeta, and the brothers lay there, their hearts pounding with exhilaration and satisfaction.

One of the brothers then suggested that perhaps the two girls would like to explore each other's bodies and the other brothers nodded eagerly.

"Would you like that Vaneeta?" master Daniel asked, even though he already knew the answer, and she nodded her head quickly.

What about you Naima? Would you like to give us a little show? Naima quickly nodded yes also.

The two girls, Naima and Vaneeta, moved towards each other with a fiery intensity born from curiosity. Their bodies collided and they wrapped their arms around each other in a passionate embrace.

As they pressed together, their breasts rubbed against one another, eliciting moans of pleasure. Vaneeta leaned in and kissed Naima's nipple, gently sucking on it as her hand snaked down to her pussy.

She tugged on the curly hair before plunging two fingers inside, causing Naima to sink to her knees in ecstasy.

With her fingers still deep within Naima, Vaneeta spread her legs even wider and pushed her to the carpeted floor, exposing the delicate folds of her pussy for all the brothers who were watching intensely to see.

She replaced her fingers with her lips and expertly explored the pink clit and wetness that awaited her there, driving both herself and Naima into a frenzy of desire.

The four brothers stood transfixed, their eyes fixed upon the intense scene unfolding before them. Their gazes were locked onto the two young women, whose bodies moved with a fiery dance.

They could see the rush of pleasure on the flushed faces, the way their breasts jiggled and swayed, and the way their hands explored. The sight alone was enough to make their own bodies ache with desire.

The scent of feminine arousal and the sharp tang of male desire blended together in a tantalizing aroma that filled the room and added to the charged atmosphere.

The taste of anticipation lingered on their tongues, a mix of need and excitement as they watched the two women pleasure each other without reservation, oblivious to their presence.

The four brothers shifted on their feet, their hands twitching with the urge to join in on the action.

Their own bodies responded to the sight before them, their cocks throbbing painfully with lust.

It was a game to see who could resist touching himself the longest, something that had been suggested by Naima who had grown bolder.

Each brother could feel his own body reacting to the intense scene before them.

Their hands fisted and their muscles tensed as they

fought against the urge to touch themselves. They could feel the heat radiating from the two women.

The tension in the room was palpable, their bodies vibrating with an electric energy as the four brothers watched the women's passions unfold.

They were like a pack of wolves, eyes wide and primal, ready to feast on the carnal display of passion before them.

The intensity of their gazes mirrored the fervor of the two women, their bodies throbbing with desire and their cocks straining as they stood out like flags on poles.

They were eager to join in on the erotic dance before them.

CHAPTER 8

The brothers couldn't control themselves any longer. With frenzied desperation, their hands reached for their throbbing members, gripping and stroking with a primal need.

The pain of their arousal was almost unbearable, but they couldn't stop, couldn't resist the overwhelming urge to touch themselves in this moment of pure desire. This was a game each of them didn't mind losing.

The two girls were lost in their own world, completely consumed by the intense pleasure they were giving and receiving from each other. It was a first for both of them, being with another woman, but it felt so natural and right.

Naima shifted Vaneeta's body until her pussy was directly over her mouth, still slick with arousal from their previous actions. Without hesitation, she pressed her lips to the wetness before her and began to suck and lick at the sensitive flesh.

Vaneeta moaned as Naima's tongue expertly explored her most intimate areas, sending waves of pleasure through her body. She couldn't believe how good it felt to have another woman pleasuring her like that.

As the two girls continued to gamahuche each other in perfect synchronization, their moans and gasps filled the room. Nothing else mattered but the intense pleasure they were experiencing.

Their bodies moved together with a primal rhythm, grinding and thrusting against each other as they chased their orgasms. Their mutual pleasure was driving them both insane .

Naima uttered a not-so-delicate groan of pleasure as she felt Vaneeta's pussy clench around her tongue, signaling her imminent orgasm.

Her own climax built up rapidly, pulsing through her body in waves of pure bliss. As she lost control, she felt Vaneeta's orgasm overtake her, their bodies convulsing in perfect syncopation.

Their orgasms shook them to the core, leaving them panting and trembling with pleasure. They collapsed onto the floor in a sweaty tangle of limbs when they came off their highs.

For a few moments, they just lay there catching their breaths as their bodies slowly relaxed from the intense releases. Vaneeta soon felt a hand on her leg that didn't belong to Naima.

She opened her eyes to see one of the brothers kneeling between her legs, his eyes dark with desire.

Master James had stepped forward, carefully pulling the spent lovers apart. His eyes never left Vaneeta's as he spoke, "We have all enjoyed the show." He smiled slyly, "Perhaps now it's our turn."

Without a word, Vaneeta and Naima each turned their attention to the men.

The women could taste each other on their lovers' lips as they took turns kissing the men, a bittersweet combination of desire and fulfillment. The salty taste only fuelled the intensity of their pleasure.

The taste of the salt and sweat lingered on their tongues as the men's mouths found the women's necks and breasts, leaving passionate marks as their bodies moved as one.

It turned out it was master Daniel was kneeling over Naima, his cock ramrod straight.

With each thrust, Vaneeta and Naima could feel the solid heat of their lovers' bodies against their own, the firmness of their strong hands gripping their hips. They were completely consumed by the sensations.

The women's bodies were slick and warm, their skin glistening with sweat as the men's hands roamed and explored, their bodies writhing together in a perfect dance of pleasure.

Vaneeta and Naima's bodies shuddered as the hard, hot cocks filled them, their skin tingling with every touch and moan.

The brothers' hands gripped their hips tightly, guiding their movements and adding to the electrifying sensation.

The men, at various times, stood at attention, like soldiers ready for battle, taking turns plunging into their women's bodies with a primal hunger that could not be denied.

The women surrendered to the relentless assault, their moans and cries echoing in the room like a melody of erotic pleasure. It became a dance of ecstasy and release, a primal and carnal display of desire and satisfaction.

One of the masters picked up some oil that was nearby and its coldness sent shivers through Vaneeta's body as it was drizzled onto her skin.

The sensation quickly turned warm and slippery as the master's hands began to massage the oil onto her ass cheeks.

Vaneeta moaned at the feeling, her body arching into his touch. She could feel herself getting wetter and hotter with each passing second, her arousal building to a fever pitch.

The master's hands roamed up and down her back, kneading and caressing with firm pressure. His fingers found their way between her cheeks, rubbing the oil into every crease and fold.

Vaneeta pushed back against the hands, wanting more of his touch. She could feel his hard cock pressing against her thigh, aching to be inside of her.

As if reading her mind, the master moved behind Vaneeta and his cock disappeared into her anus in one smooth motion.

Vaneeta cried out at the feeling of being filled so completely, the combination of the oil and his hard cock sending jolts of pleasure through her body.

He gripped onto Vaneeta's hips tightly as he thrusts into her relentlessly, each movement causing waves of pleasure to course through Vaneeta's body.

She reached back to grab onto his thighs for support as she matched his movements, their bodies moving together in perfect harmony.

Meanwhile, Naima was being pleasured by two brothers at once. One brother had positioned himself behind her while the other's cock was plunging in and out of her mouth with wild abandon.

The two men worked together in perfect unison, with one on his back, thrusting deep inside her pussy while the other caressed and teased every inch of Naima's sensitive skin before invading her puckered lips with is shaft.

Naima was in ecstasy as she swallowed one cock while being filled from behind by another. Her body shook with pleasure as they moved against each other in perfect rhythm. A third brother moved over from Vaneeta to join them.

He squirted some oil on her buttocks and massaged it as he drooled. Her eyes grew wide because she knew they would do what was being done to Vaneeta, breach her chocolate pot.

She was afraid and felt her anal glands clench. However, the feeling of the oil and the fingers that were then stretching her sphincter lessened her fear, plus, she had seen the look of pure joy on Vaneeta's face.

Once they felt Naima was sufficiently ready, one lucky brother now moved in, clamped his cock between her butt cheeks and slid up and down to lubricate his weapon before spreading her anus wider with his fingers.

He started with one, and when she got comfortable with it, added more calloused fingers.

He burrowed himself slowly into her butthole after she started wriggling back against his engulfed digits, wanting more.

He withdrew them and gloated with pleasure at the rosebud he was about to initiate into anal sex.

There was less resistance of the anal sphincter as it welcomed his charger.

Before long, his cock was deep in her entrails and his ball banged against her butt cheeks.

*** Naima***

Naima's eyes grew wide and the fear in them was evident, and her pupils dilated with uncertainty.

The brothers' hands were slick with oil as they stretched her sphincter, their fingers glistening in the dimly lit room.

She felt the oil being massaged onto her buttocks and the fingers stretching her anus, she also felt her muscles clench in fear. But, the feeling of relaxation and pleasure from the massage lessened her fear.

The fingers spread her anus wider. Her gaze flickered between Vaneeta's face, filled with pure joy, and a brother's face, filled with desire.

Her body tensed as she felt the fingers stretching and preparing her for penetration. The oil slick on her skin and the slight pressure of the fingers against her most sensitive flesh.

The anal glands clenched in anticipation, her body tense as she waited for their next move.

The brothers' fingers were firm yet gentle as they worked to prepare her pliant ass cheeks.

The feeling of being penetrated from behind and

having her anus stretched caused a mixture of fear and pleasure to race through her.

He withdrew his fingers and placed the slick head of his cock at her entrance. She felt a slight resistance as he pushed inside, something one of her brothers had warned her about.

He paused until she relaxed and then slowly inched his way deeper, grunting and whispering words of encouragement as he filled her completely.

The feeling that took over was indescribable as she enjoyed the feeling of being anally fucked.

Unwittingly, she had displaced the brother in her pussy who instead, licked her while he stretched her cunt lips farther.

He was on his back with his cock standing straight up while his brother pushed down on her body to direct her pussy to the waiting cock which impaled her.

She screamed with joy as she felt the two brothers inside her at the same time. The other two brothers moved towards them and they again impaled Vaneeta. The two girls kissed and caressed each other while being doubly penetrated

He slowly withdrew his fingers from her and guided the head of his erection to her entrance. She felt a slight resistance, reminiscent of the warnings her brothers had given her about this kind of pleasure. He paused until she relaxed before slowly pushing himself inside, grunting and whispering encouragements as he filled her completely.

As he moved within her, she was overcome with indescribable sensations. But then, something unexpected happened. One of her brothers, who had been watching nearby, couldn't resist joining in on the fun. He licked at her exposed cunt flesh while his brother continued to thrust into her from behind.

Then came pure ecstasy when Naima found herself being penetrated by two brothers at once, one deep in her pussy while the other was heated in her asshole.

She screamed with delight as they both took turns pleasuring her, their bodies moving in harmony as they shared this intimate moment together.

Meanwhile, the other two brothers went with Vaneeta, who was also eagerly awaiting their touch. They entered her simultaneously, causing her to moan and writhe in pleasure.

The two girls embraced and kissed each other passionately, kneading their jiggly breasts that bounced up and down as they were doubly penetrated by the four brothers.

The night wore on and the brothers continued to take turns pleasuring Naima and Vaneeta. They moved from one girl to the other, each taking their turn to indulge in every available hole.

At one point, they positioned the two girls side by side on the edge of the bed with their legs splayed open.

The brothers took turns plunging into one pussy, then quickly switching to the other and repeating until both girls were moaning and writhing with pleasure. Sometimes, it was pussy, then pussy, sometimes, pussy, then asshole, and sometimes ass and ass. It was like a childhood game, only with wanton pleasures.

The lively and willing girls cheered them on, encouraging them to go faster and harder. And the brothers were happy to oblige, taking turns between each girl and sharing their bodies equally.

They indulged in every pleasure imaginable - from oral sex to anal play, delighting in every sensation as they explored each other's bodies. None held back, giving in to their desires completely.

It was a night that they would never forget, filled with intense pleasure and a sense of forbidden excitement. To the girls, nothing else mattered but the overwhelming sensation of being completely filled and loved by these four men.

Sometimes the girls would eat each other's pussy while being impaled by one brother or another. None of their holes went unfilled.

Naima was treated better than she had ever been by her master after the pleasure filled night.

"If he ever treats you badly, girlie, you can always come here," master Daniel teased to which his brother replied: "Never without me." His voice was gruff, but his brothers knew he was joking.

The two slave girls had made their brotherly bond much stronger.

It would go on to the first of many enjoyable family reunions with Vaneeta and Naima being the objects of attraction and devotion in that old plantation.

THANK YOU

Thank you for your purchase of this collection. You can sign up to my mailing list to receive notification whenever a new book releases.

If you enjoyed it, I would appreciate a customer review.

Join here: or scan with your phone:

ABOUT THE AUTHOR

Sage Dearly is an emerging author of smutty romance shorts of all sorts with her historical shorts light on history.

She has dreamt of writing since she was a youngster when she accidentally happened upon sexually explicit books at a basement bookstore.

Now, she's finally living that dream and loving it. You can support her by buying direct on her website and subscribing to the newsletter.

Sage's website

In the heart of the antebellum South, Kwame, a newly arrived slave to the sprawling southern plantation, finds himself thrust into a delicate dance of desire and power.

Caught in the gaze of the lady of the house, he is swiftly reassigned to her quarters, a shift that promises opportunity.

When the master of the plantation is away, he leaves the vast estate momentarily unguarded and the lady seizes her chance.

Amidst the flickering flames of forbidden passion, another presence lingers—the lady's daughter, a young woman torn between curiosity and jealousy as she watches their clandestine affair unfold.

For Kwame, the allure of female companionship is a beacon of solace in the oppressive shadows of servitude, igniting a fire within him that drives him to navigate the treacherous waters of plantation life with cunning and determination.

Naughty Noon Tales: Marcia

Marcia is a lonely and restless housewife whose mundane world takes an unexpected turn in the intoxicating heat of "Naughty Noon Tales."

When a substitute gardener tends to more than just her garden, she finds herself entangled in a web of desire and forbidden passion.

The clock ticks towards noon and Marcia succumbs to a liaison that is quite different from her predictable life.

In the sultry haze of midday, Marcia's confession unfolds. You don't want to miss this seductive confession.

Click Here

Vaneeta's life at the plantation is about to change when she meets the plantation owner's twin brother who's there to celebrate their birthday.

Amid all the preparations, she is eager to give them her special present. An exceptional night for the threesome and there was no going back once she experienced the exquisite pleasure of the flesh.

Her life lesson continues when the other brothers come to visit and partake in the sexual awakening in the sequential books that can be read as stand-alone also.

Buy Them Here

You can also find her books on your favorite online platforms.